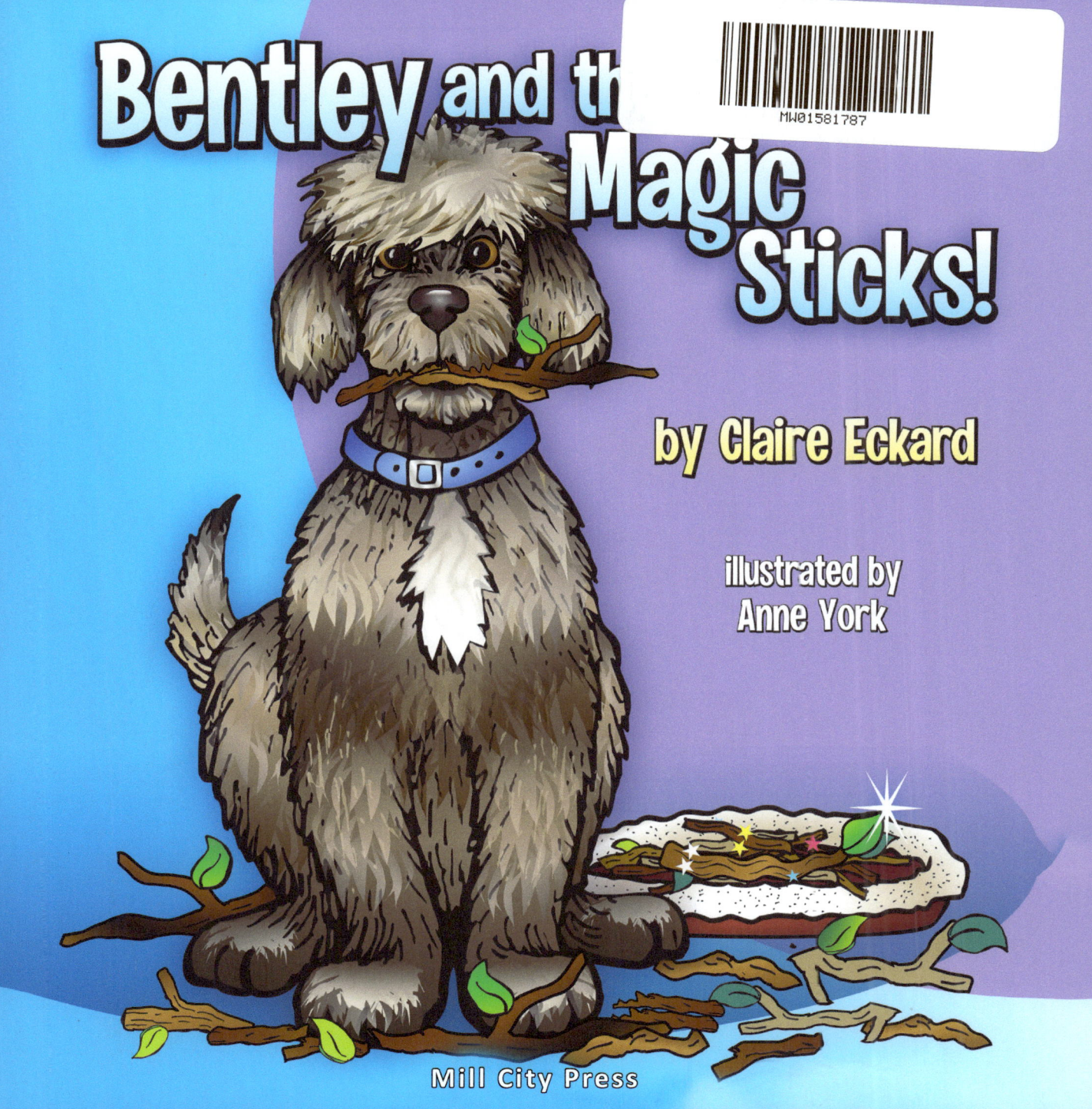

Mill City Press, Inc.
2301 Lucien Way #415
Maitland, FL 32751
407.339.4217
www.millcitypress.net

© 2021 by Author: CLAIRE ECKARD
Illustrated by Anne York

All rights reserved. No part of this publication may be reproduced, stored in a retrieval system, or transmitted, in any form or by any means, electronic, mechanical, photocopying, recording, or otherwise, without the prior written permission of the author.

Printed in the United States of America

Paperback ISBN-13: 978-1-6628-1038-1
Hard Cover ISBN-13: 978-1-6628-1039-8
Ebook ISBN-13: 978-1-6628-1040-4

It was hard for Bentley to fit into a lot of places because he was so BIG.

When he was a puppy he had a lovely dog bed to sleep in.

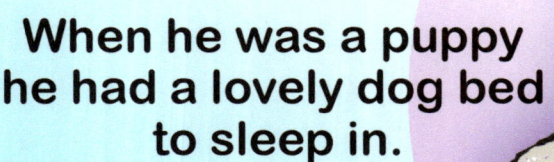

But now he was all grown up it was WAAAAYY too small for him!

His legs fell over the edges, and his head ended up on the floor.

Bentley loved going for walks to the park with his human, but ever since he had grown SOOOO big the other dogs would run away from him. Their humans even ran away as well!

Just because Bentley was big didn't mean that he would hurt anyone. Not on purpose anyway!

Poor Bentley didn't have any friends. He was very sad. He spent a lot of time alone because he didn't have anyone to play with. He would just lay in the dog park with his favorite stick watching all the other dogs play together. His human felt very sad for him. He knew that Bentley wanted to be like all the other dogs and not be left out just because he looked different.

The one thing that made Bentley happy was STICKS! He collected big sticks, little sticks, medium-sized sticks, and even sticks with things sticking out of them!

Bentley loved his sticks. Bentley thought of the sticks as his friends since he didn't have any real friends of his own. He kept all his sticks in his dog bed.
(He couldn't fit in there anyway!)

Bentley was very grateful
for all that he DID have.
He had a lovely human, a great dog bed,
and he was sure that his stick collection
was the best in the world!
Every morning he would
wake up and say to himself
"Good morning world!"
and then he would turn to
his sticks and say"
Good morning sticks!"

Bentley's dog bowl was FOUR times the size of a normal dog bowl, and his water bowl was a very large bucket!

Bentley always ate a HUGE breakfast, because when you are as big as Bentley you need a lot of food!

After breakfast Bentley would go and explore the garden at his house.

He would sniff all around the edges to make sure no new smells had appeared overnight that needed investigating. Then he would lay down in his favorite spot where he could watch the lizards running around and the insects busily going about their business. Before long he would be fast asleep!

Every day, when his human came home from work, he would take Bentley for a walk to the dog park.

On the way to the dog park Bentley would pick up the newspapers laying in the humans' driveways and take them all the way to the front door so they didn't have to walk so far to pick them up.

Then, when Bentley got to the dog park, he would very carefully pick up any trash he saw lying on the grass. He would put it into the trash can so the park would look beautiful for all the pets and their humans to enjoy. Bentley was such a good dog!

When he
got back from the park,
Bentley would eat a very LARGE dinner, and then he
would bring his human a nice cozy pair of slippers and they
would settle down to watch their favorite shows on television.
Bentley loved his life, although he was a little
lonely sometimes with no friends to play with.

One night, a very strange thing happened.
A magical, wonderful, mystical, SUPER-COOL thing! A Fairy DogMother, named Tia, visited Bentley's house while he was sleeping!
Tia knew that Bentley was lonely, and she wanted to use her fairy magic to help him feel better.

While Bentley was sleeping Tia waved her tail over Bentley's pile of sticks.

"Magic tail, wag and shake
Fairy dust will magic make!
Close your eyes and count to TEN,
Now make Bentley a new friend!!"

As Tia sprinkled fairy dust
from her magic tail, the
sticks in Bentley's dog bed
started moving,
and squirming,
and shape-shifting,
and bending,
and wrapping themselves
around each other,
and OH MY GOODNESS!
Look what happened!
Do you see what I see?

In the morning, Bentley opened his eyes and did a big stretch. "Good morning, world," he said as usual. "Good morning, sticks!"

Then Bentley sat up, stretched, and got ready to count his sticks, but OH MY! Laying in his bed, sound asleep and SNORING, was another dog; a dog that was made of STICKS!!!

Bentley was not sure what to make of it!
He sniffed the strange creature.
It smelled just like his very own pile of sticks!
Just then the Stick-Dog woke up.

He stretched (just like Bentley had) and
very matter-of-factly said,
"Good morning, Bentley.
My name is Sticky! Did you sleep well?"

Bentley's eyes grew large and round. He decided he MUST still be asleep and dreaming! He walked over to his very large water bucket and stuck his head ALL the way in it. Once he was sure he was awake, he pulled his head out, shook all the extra water off, and looked around to see if Sticky was still there.

Sticky was standing up and was eating breakfast out of Bentley's dog bowl!
"Come on, Bentley" Sticky said between bites,
"You need to eat breakfast as well. We have a busy day ahead!"

"We do?" asked Bentley, surprised. He couldn't remember the last time he had a busy day! That sounded like fun! So he started to tuck into his breakfast right alongside Sticky. It was the first time he had EVER had someone to share a meal with!

In between bites, Bentley asked Sticky where he was from. "Tia, your Fairy Dogmother, made me so that you would have a friend to play with!" said Sticky. Bentley was VERY excited to have a friend to play with and was even MORE excited that he had a Fairy Dogmother! He wondered if he would ever get to meet her in person!

Bentley and Sticky had a wonderful day sniffing around the garden and taking a nap under the tree, and Bentley even showed Sticky where he had hidden all his favorite bones! It was Bentley's **BEST DAY EVER!!**

When it was time for the human to take Bentley for his walk, Sticky came right along with them. Bentley carried Sticky to the park on his back! Luckily, most humans can't see magic, so Bentley's human didn't notice Sticky at all. Sticky just looked like a plain old stick to him. Unfortunately, though, the other dogs at the park COULD see Sticky and were very curious about Bentley's new friend.

Freddie,
an old English sheepdog,
came running over to Bentley and asked,
"What do you have there, Bentley?
Can I take a look?"
Freddie had never wanted to play with him before,
however Bentley was far too nice to be mean to
Freddie, so he told him he could take a look at
Sticky if he was VERY, VERY careful.

Freddie leaned over and sniffed Sticky all over. Sticky didn't smell like anything Freddie had ever sniffed before. Freddie lifted his head and barked across the field to a fluffy St. Bernard puppy named Zeus.
"Hey Zeus, come over here and sniff this!" he yelled.
Zeus came running over to see what all the fuss was about. He was followed by Stetson the Dachshund, Rachel the Poodle, and Rex the Blue Heeler!
Soon they were all sniffing poor Sticky!

**Now you must remember
what dogs usually do to sticks.
They carry them around in their
wet slobbery mouths, and then they
CHEW THEM UP!!!
Suddenly the worst, most unthinkable thing
that could ever happen, happened!
The human, thinking Bentley had finally
made some new friends to play with, walked
over to the group of dogs, grabbed Sticky by
the legs, and threw him as far as he could!!
"Fetch the stick, Bentley," he shouted!**

As Sticky flew through the air, ALL the dogs started madly dashing across the grass after him. Bentley lumbered after them as fast as he could! He was so big that it was hard to run fast!

But it was too late. As Sticky fell to the ground he shattered into a pile of plain, dirty old sticks. Each of the dogs grabbed a stick and ran away with it.

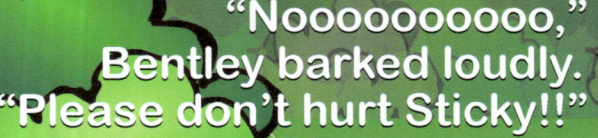
"Nooooooooooo," Bentley barked loudly. "Please don't hurt Sticky!!"

By the time Bentley reached his friend, only Sticky's tail was left lying on the ground.
Bentley sat down next to the tail and howled and howled sadly. His howls echoed around the park. They were the saddest howls anyone had EVER heard.

Finally, Bentley picked up Sticky's tail and carried it home where he gently laid it in his dog bed. Exhausted, Bentley laid down and slept next to what was left of his BEST and ONLY friend.

Tia waved her magic tail and showed the dogs an image of Bentley laying sadly at home next to his last and only stick. When they saw how sad Bentley looked they all felt even worse.
"You are all going to have to find a way to make it up to Bentley and tell him you are sorry," she said.
"The biggest thing about Bentley is his heart. If you all go and apologize to him I know he will forgive you."

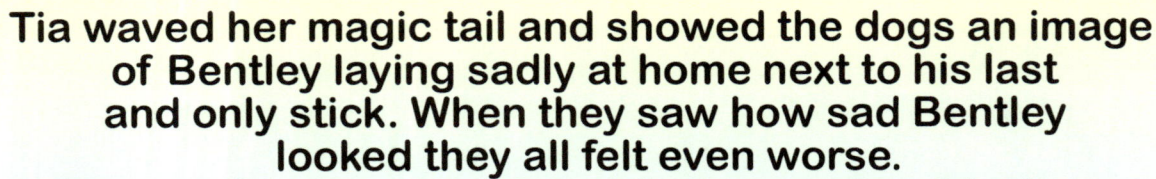

Just before dark, Bentley heard barking outside the front door. Sitting on the doorstep were Freddie, Stetson, Rachel, Rex, and Zeus. Laying in front of each of them was a stick, slightly drooled on and lightly chewed, but otherwise none the worse for wear!

"Bentley, we feel very badly about running off with your special sticks," said Rachel. "We are so sorry, and we have brought them all back for you. Will you consider being our friend?"
Bentley could not believe his eyes!
All the dogs seemed very sorry for what they had done, and they had brought every single stick back to him.

"I know I am really big and might seem a little scary, but all I ever really wanted was to be friends with all of you." Bentley told the group. He carefully put all the sticks back into his dog bed. Then he invited his new friends into his garden for a game of Find-The-Bone (He was very good at hiding bones and was pretty sure they would never find it!!).

That night, Bentley fell asleep next to his bed full of all the sticks that used to be Sticky. He was happy he had lots of new friends, but really missed his first and most special friend. While he was fast asleep Tia quietly appeared and waved her magic tail over one VERY special stick. Then she hid a letter under Bentley's bed and blew a magical kiss over Bentley as he slept!

When he woke up in the morning, Bentley noticed that the stick that had once been Sticky's tail was all SHINY and SPARKLY. Bentley noticed a piece of paper peeking out from under the edge of the dog bed. He used his nose to push the dog bed away and there he found the letter. Not just any old letter, but a sparkly, beautiful, wonderful letter covered in MAGIC fairy dust!

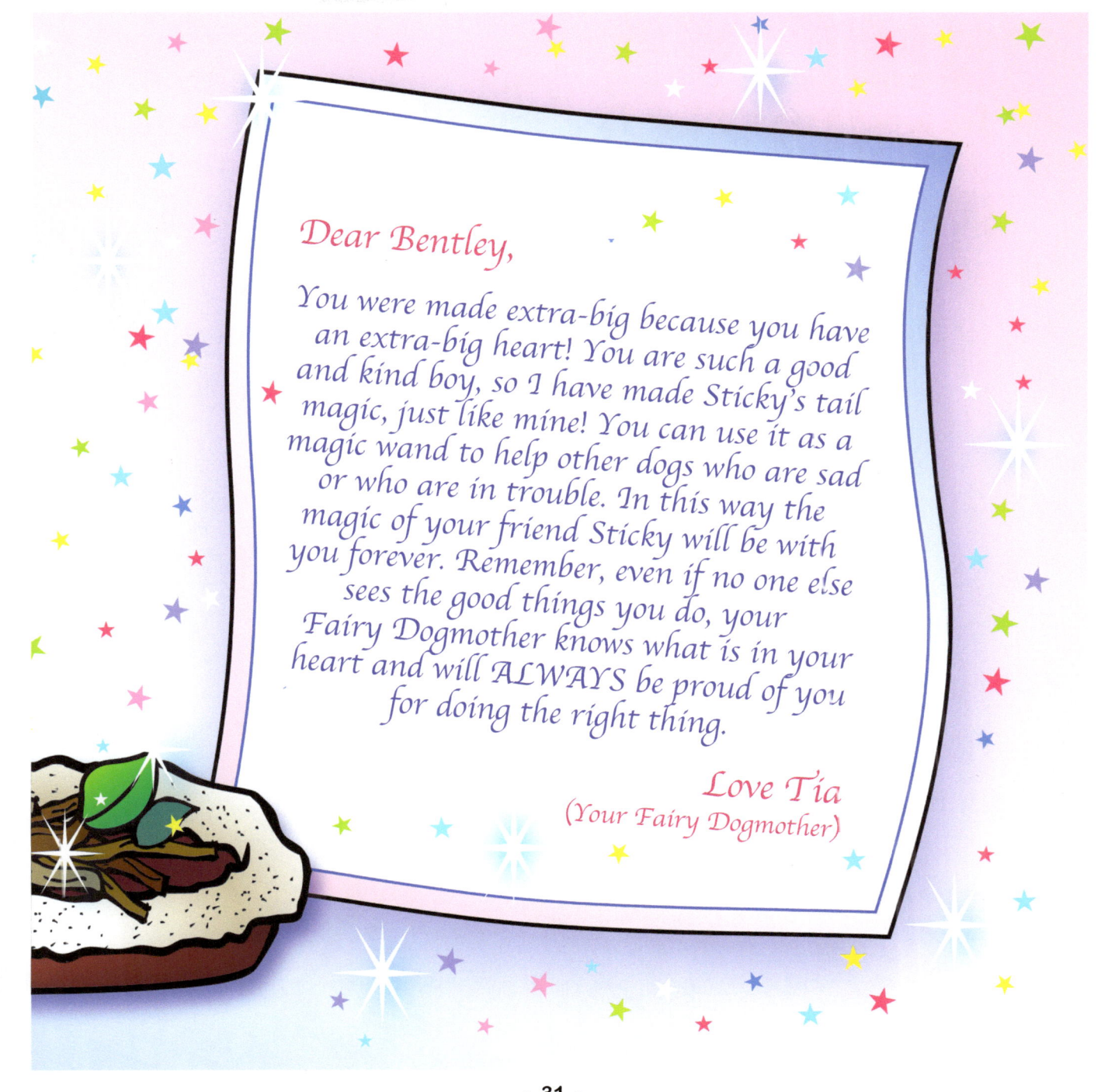

Dear Bentley,

You were made extra-big because you have an extra-big heart! You are such a good and kind boy, so I have made Sticky's tail magic, just like mine! You can use it as a magic wand to help other dogs who are sad or who are in trouble. In this way the magic of your friend Sticky will be with you forever. Remember, even if no one else sees the good things you do, your Fairy Dogmother knows what is in your heart and will ALWAYS be proud of you for doing the right thing.

Love Tia
(Your Fairy Dogmother)

Bentley was SO happy. With Sticky's magic tail he would be able to help lots of other dogs. And now Bentley also knew WHY he had grown so big; it was to make room for his big, kind heart!

Bentley had a very large heart.
In fact, he had an ENORMOUS heart.
Think of the biggest heart you can imagine; well Bentley's was

BIGGER!!!!

(and now he also had a magic tail!!!!)

the end

Claire Eckard
Author

Claire Eckard is an animal lover, and especially enjoys her three rescue dogs, one of whom is the star of this book! Claire is an author, songwriter, and poet. She lives in Prescott, Arizona with her husband, dogs, horses and a rambunctious miniature mule. She adores her two grown sons, her daughter in law, and her two Granddaughters who inspire her to write heartwarming children's stories with a few life lessons thrown in for good measure!

Anne York
Illustrator

Anne lives in rural Southern California, sharing her small ranch with her 5 dogs, 3 horses, 2 cats and a goat, so there is never a lack of inspiration for her characters. Trained as a graphic artist, she is always thrilled when there is an animal theme! When not working Anne enjoys horseback riding, backpacking and creating ceramics with equine designs.

CPSIA information can be obtained
at www.ICGtesting.com
Printed in the USA
BVHW020002070421
604324BV00010B/51